BROTHERS FOREVER

STORY & PICTURES BY CLAUDIA BOLDT

JONATHAN CAPE • LONDON

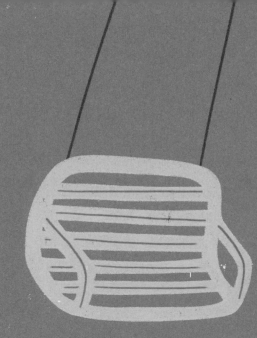

JONATHAN CAPE

UK | USA | Canada | Ireland | Australia
India | New Zealand | South Africa
Jonathan Cape is part of the Penguin Random House
group of companies whose addresses can be found at
global.penguinrandomhouse.com.
www.penguin.co.uk
www.puffin.co.uk
www.ladybird.co.uk

 Penguin
Random House
UK

First published 2018
001

Printed in China

A CIP catalogue record for this book is
available from the British Library

ISBN: 978-1-780-08033-8

All correspondence to:
Jonathan Cape, Penguin Random House Children's
80 Strand, London WC2R 0RL

 MIX
Paper from
responsible sources
FSC® C018179

Some days you think you have it all.

Barney is my big brother
and my best friend.

We bake cakes.

We plant trees.

We play hide-and-seek.

We dance.

We draw together.

I'm sure it'll be this way forever.

Tomorrow is Barney's first day at school.

He is all excited and I keep him company.
It's hard to fall asleep when you are all excited.

"I'll tell you all about it," says Barney.
"Promise?" I ask.
"Promise!" says Barney.

While Barney is at school
I go about my day as usual.
But my cake tastes sad,

my drawings look gloomy

and there is no one to hide from.

I never knew a day could be so long.

Little did I know that from now on
Barney has very important things to do.

"And it's Barnaby now.
B-A-R-N-A-B-Y."

His new friends seem to be
more interesting than me.

Sometimes I'm allowed to play with them.

But it's never any fun.

I really want to be
best friends again.

But I don't know what
to say any more.

A bear's got to know when to give it up.

So I make a new friend.

His name is Podgy.

We bake cakes.

We plant trees.

We play hide-and-seek.

We dance.

We draw together.

The others snicker when they see us.
They say Podgy's just a toy and not a friend.

Podgy's not impressed.
And who could blame him?
I had enough a long time ago.

One day I notice something funny
about Barney.
He doesn't want his ice cream.
Something is always up when
Barney doesn't eat his ice cream.

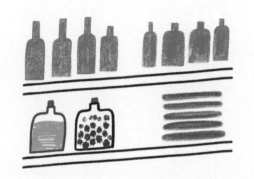

That night Barney knocks on my door.

Barney crawls into my bed like he used to.
Except now we have a little less space
with Podgy here too.

Tomorrow Barney is leaving on a school trip.
He has never been away from home before.
"I'll miss you," he says. He is sorry too.
I think about it for a minute.

Then I say that Barney can take Podgy.

Now Barney won't be homesick at all.

Podgy will love it too.

Barney promised to tell me all about his trip.
I can't wait for him to come back.

And when Barney comes home
he is really happy to see me.

Barney tells me everything about
their great adventure.
It's as if I'd been there too.

Podgy fitted right in.

He even met a lovely
sausage dog.

Things are changing all the time
but brothers are forever.